MYSTERY OF THE MASTER SUITE

A HAYWARD HALL SHORT STORY

ALEXANDRIA BLAELOCK

BlueMere Books
MELBOURNE, AUSTRALIA

For permission requests, please contact
enquiries@bluemerebooks.com.

Ordering Information:
Discounts are available on quantity purchases. For details, contact orders@bluemerebooks.com.

The Mystery of the Master Suite/Alexandria Blaelock
paperback ISBN: 978-1-925749-58-8
digital ISBN: 978-1-925749-59-5

Book Layout © BookDesignTemplates.com

MYSTERY OF
THE MASTER SUITE

If there is one thing that almost everyone who has ever been married knows, it's that the lead up to the day is terrifying and exhilarating by turns.

While there is a special thrill to be had by attending Church to hear the banns being read, and the congregation praying for you, it doesn't really do much for your peace of mind.

Except perhaps for that five minutes when everyone's calming thoughts are focused on you.

But the minute you leave the building, it's back to worrying about the arrangements.

And in this respect, Miss Morag Clementine, late of twenty-first-century Melbourne worried about them a lot less than her fiancé Mr Henry Fox, and her mother-in-law to be, who were much more invested in the proprieties.

After all, it was the year 1905, and they had reputations to maintain.

In the nine months since Morag'd arrived with no warning, and no logical explanation, her short, dark, red hair had grown into the kind of bob that wouldn't become fashionable for another ten years or so.

She'd relaxed into floor-length skirts, and the hair on her legs was almost as luxuriant as that on her head.

Morag summarily rejected the tightly corseted S-curve silhouette of the Gibson Girl and embraced the two-piece walking ensemble of trumpet skirt and blouse.

She was particularly fond of a tightly tailored jacket, and thankfully our dressmaker was exceptional at tailoring.

This was the outfit she could be seen *running* around the gardens in, often accompanied by Dante the pug, and sometimes by fiance Henry Fox who had trouble keeping up with her.

Our Henry, it has to be said, being a man of his time, was rather too fond of rich food and too much wine.

She first met her groom in 2020, coincidentally in the same house as she was living in 1905. She hadn't realised how fond she was of future Henry until she'd left him.

At his insistence.

By going back to the day he'd got lost in time to prevent him from triggering the event.

Through which method she'd lost that Henry by becoming stuck in time herself.

With our present-day...

Or maybe her past Henry.

Or, seeing as she was marrying him, maybe even her future Henry.

Time paradoxes can be quite hard to get your head around.

There was no doubt in her mind, that the 1905 version of Henry was the better looking of the two, mainly because he didn't carry the cares of a century with him.

But also, because his perfectly ordinary brown hair and eyes seemed much brighter by contrast with his lush reddish-brown moustache.

Though without the exposure to other ideas and cultures, he could be a little, well, backwards. Or to put it more charitably, traditional.

Being possibly the most modern of modern women at that time, she'd moved into the Master suite almost before he'd asked her to stay with him. And made him bring her in a tiny desk she'd found in the attic so she could sit at it in the big bay window.

I'm not sure she truly believed she had "fixed" him; that he was fully anchored in time with her instead of travelling to a different time and place every day.

I think she wanted to be there to make sure our Henry stayed in 1905 with her. Or at the very least, that he couldn't leave without her.

Though to be honest, it sounds to me that travelling to a different place every day might be better than staying in the stifling atmosphere of Hayward Hall.

Morag would've been perfectly happy without a wedding, but scandalised, our family wasn't having any of that.

Like I say, she was very modern. I for one found her refusal to accept any limitations inspiring.

So, the wedding was on, but they couldn't persuade her to observe the proprieties and move back out of his rooms.

The last of the banns had been read, and she was facing her last week of singledom.

Bearing in mind how... let's say tense, she became when he tried to discuss any of the more feminine arts with her, he'd screwed up his courage and suggested she might like to redecorate the house.

Morag assured him the heavy mahogany furniture would be worth a fortune one day, (presumably, she knew that for a fact). Not to mention that she adored its "retro effect" (whatever that was) and that the suite was large enough to render said furniture small by comparison.

However, given the opportunity, she would adore a nice blue Chinoiserie wallpaper.

Okay, that's not exactly what she said, but half the time we didn't know what she was talking about.

Except when it came to the coffee.

The late nineteenth-century coffee craze had largely passed us by, but Morag was barely civil without several cups of it in the morning.

She liked it in a big cup of warm milk, which we found fascinating, and which was unbelievably delicious.

As the day of the wedding grew closer and closer, Morag started taking longer and longer runs to calm her nerves.

And spending more and more time in the library, busily reading books and newspapers to catch up on current events, fashion and etiquette.

Morag particularly liked looking at the spreads in the society pages about Henry and her.

She'd lean on her arm, and look at the photographs and say, "imagine that, some chick from Footscray marrying the most eligible bachelor of the decade."

She practised her gossiping on us and it was hilarious. She hadn't come from a large family like ours, and we could tell she was trying to fit in with us, and with 1905.

One time I heard her crying with the stress of it.

The day of Wednesday, August 30, 1905, dawned bitterly cold, squally and showery. In some small towns 20 miles or so out of the city, snow falls as much as two feet had been recorded.

The wedding was of course at the old St Clements in Elsternwick, not the new brick one, but the wooden one that was there before it. With the Reverend George Sproule presiding. It was a very modest affair, with only close friends and family in attendance.

You could give or take Henry in his morning suit, but Morag was radiant and beautiful.

She'd designed her own gown, cream, with a lace V neck cross-over bodice and a heavy satin notched skirt, though she said she copied someone called Jeanne Paquin.

A reception was to be held at the house, and Mama had made a special effort to decorate the ballroom with garlands of white roses from the garden.

Not herself obviously, but she directed it.

The original plan was to pose for some photographs in the garden, but that was out of the question with the weather.

Mr Smythe, the head gardener, shared Morag's interest in orchids and had decorated the conservatory with orchids and ferns.

It made a splendid backdrop for the photographs.

They did make a beautiful couple, even in the massive family shots.

And the slightly awkward shots with the servants.

You could tell they were deeply in love.

When the prints came out, they were spectacular.

Morag excused herself to freshen up before the dinner.

Henry kissed her neck because she'd already started walking towards the stairs, "hurry back," he called after her.

She turned and smiled, and in her characteristic style, she said, "oh, *I* will."

The photographer took some more pictures of the family, and the conservatory, and the rainy weather, and after a while, our Henry started looking at his watch.

And it wasn't too long before he said, "Amelia, go check on her," and because I was curious, I did.

Instead of back-chatting him.

I suppose I should mention that at this point, I was just his fifteen-year-old sister. Third youngest in the family, and usually confined to the nursery with the twins.

Dante, who by this point was more Morag's dog than Mama's, came haring after me.

I did a quick swoop through the ground floor rooms, though I didn't call her name as the guests were already assembling and I didn't want to alarm them.

Then I ran upstairs and I heard her screaming.

Not a short, sharp scream like a girl might make when you sneak up on her.

Or the kind of long, drawn-out scream you might make when you're attacked by something.

But the sort of grunting sound Morag makes when she's practising her unarmed combat.

Plus, I could hear the sounds of a scuffle, so I ran towards the Master suite, calling her name.

Dante, barking furiously, beat me to the closed door.

I heard her say, "No! Wait. I need..."

And when we burst in the door a few seconds later there was no one there.

Not Morag, and not the person she was asking to wait.

Her chair had been knocked over, the top of her desk was empty, and papers were spread all around the desk as if she'd been grasping at it for something to hold on to.

The beautiful, engraved silver fountain pen Henry gave her as an engagement gift was on the other side of the room.

As if she'd thrown it at her attacker to deflect them.

The net curtains waved wildly in the stiff breeze through the window.

Though seeing as she always had the windows open, no matter the weather, I ignored them.

Dante ran around the room, barking his way through the dressing room and onto the bathroom, and I followed him calling her name.

She didn't answer, and there was no sign of her.

On our way back, I opened the bathroom and dressing room doors but didn't see anyone, or anything suspicious in either corridor.

Dante spent a lot of time sniffing around her desk and trotting from window to window whining.

With nothing else to go on, I looked out of the windows.

The ground floor had a roofed verandah underneath so, it would have been possible to climb out the window, crawl across the roof, then shimmy down a column to the ground.

At least it was possible to do all that from the nursery window so I saw no reason to doubt it was possible from the master.

But I didn't see how you could make Morag do that without a fight.

And a great deal of noise.

Unless she was unconscious.

I couldn't see anything on the ground from my vantage point.

A shiver ran down my spine, not just from the cold wind.

There was nothing for it, but to tell Henry his bride was missing.

Dante refused to leave the room. He lay down under the desk, back to the room, resting his nose on his paws.

Henry didn't take the news well.

"That's not possible," he said, "I don't believe it."

And ran through the house, ignoring well-wishers, and up the stairs. Ignoring Dante, he conducted his own search of the suite.

I waited on his bed.

He slumped down beside me, running his fingers through his hair.

"She can't be gone," he said, looking hopefully at me.

I didn't know what to do, so I shrugged.

Henry started crying like a girl.

Shortly after that Roberts, Henry's valet arrived.

"Henry, what's wrong?"

Henry blubbered something, and Roberts looked at me to translate.

"Morag's gone missing. I heard her call out just before I came in."

He looked around the room, and Henry, mostly useless on the bed.

Roberts clearly had no idea what to do either.

"Right," I said, "you find Barnes, tell him what's happened, and ask him to telephone the police. I'll find Nanny and see if she has a syrup or something that might help Henry."

Roberts tugged his vest down, squared his shoulders and nodded.

We went our separate ways.

By the time I had found Nanny, convinced her to leave the twins on their best behaviour, helped her find the laudanum, and got back to Henry, he was asleep, curled up on the bed with Dante.

I left Nanny with him, then went back downstairs to tell the rest of the family.

About the time they'd got over, "I don't believe it," and "It's impossible," Barnes announced, "the Police are on their way."

Mama managed to get a grip on herself, saying "let's go into the Drawing Room to wait." And asking Barnes, "would you please fetch us all a tot of whisky for the shock?"

Barnes came to me last and looked at me for what seemed like a very long time before he gave me a tiny slosh in a glass.

I was already thinking five steps ahead of everyone else, and I asked him, "have you been checking the guests off the list as they arrived?"

He looked at me a bit more, frowning.

Or maybe thinking.

They don't call me Trouble for nothing.

"No. We've been rushing the guests through into the ballroom, and directing the cars onto the gravel."

"So, there's no real way to be sure who's here and who isn't? Or whether we have any wedding crashers?"

"Our servants would recognise many of the guests, but I suppose it can't be ruled out."

The photographer had been hired to take pictures of the family, not the reception. But he was still hanging around in the conservatory, not quite sure what to do with himself given the news.

Barnes looked at me like he knew what I was thinking.

I threw the drink back like I'd seen Morag do, and eyes watering, managed to breathe out the fumes without squeaking.

"Quite," said Barnes

A moment later, I felt nicely relaxed, but as if my brain was working overtime.

The way I saw it, we had about 260 suspects in the house; the wedding guests and the five footmen hired to help out at the wedding.

I went back to the photographer and told him Mama had asked him to take photos of the guests. I escorted him to the ballroom; he couldn't seem to believe his luck and set up the camera and started taking pictures.

Now that I'd taken care of identifying the guests as far as possible, there were two others with histories that I knew of.

Miss Viola Seagrove who had been sent from the house in disgrace after she'd attacked Henry with a kitchen knife.

And Mr Edward Curry, Henry's former best friend, who'd decided Morag was a gold digger and set out to prove it.

I couldn't do anything about those two, except make sure the police were aware of them when they arrived.

Being only fifteen, I had read too many detective novels and had formed the opinion that all detectives were either geniuses like

Sherlock Holmes or less than intellectually gifted like Inspector Lestrade.

And sadly, Inspector Morrison of St Kilda station, a portly man with a very tall top hat, turned out to be the latter.

In those days, children were supposed to be seen and not heard, though more often than not, it was that people chose not to see or hear them. Though of course the twins and I would hang around collecting other people's secrets.

Anyway, Inspector Morrison considered a fifteen-year-old girl, with her nose stuck in a book to be of such little note that he very didn't bother to chase me away from the library where he conducted the interviews.

And I eavesdropped shamelessly.

I'm not altogether convinced Morag would have approved, but it seemed the only way I could get to the bottom of the situation was to conduct my own investigation.

The first of Inspector Morrison's shortcomings was his starting assumption that Morag had "probably been overcome with emotion and run away."

Mama and my siblings were outraged at the suggestion, talking at cross purposes over each other.

Why for heaven's sake we wondered?

Why would she do it *after* the ceremony when clearly Morag would have just said no if she didn't want to get married.

Especially in that weather.

Admittedly I wasn't a hardboiled detective by any means, but I just couldn't see what was to be gained by a woman lighting out of a place within an hour of her wedding.

It wasn't until Barnes brought her coat into the Drawing Room that Inspector Morrison was persuaded she hadn't voluntarily left the house.

The Inspector's second shortcoming was that he saw no need to comb the gardens for clues.

Admittedly he had brought only one other officer with him, and it was raining cats and dogs, but it seemed he still wanted to believe Morag had left of her own volition.

Poor kidnapped Morag could have been knocked out and secreted in one of the dozens of sheds, glasshouses and other storage places across 30 acres of ground.

When I made the suggestion, Mr Smythe was only too happy to send gardeners out walking the paths and checking the structures for any signs of Morag.

To be honest, I didn't have much hope, the weather would wash out all but the most determined steps. But my main concern was to be sure she wasn't being held on the property.

And if she was, to bring her back into the house as soon as possible.

Not to mention that there might be some other kind of suspicious behaviour.

Miss Seagrove or Mr Curry might have found their way onto the property, but not been seen by anyone at the house.

The way the Inspector Morrison saw it, there were twenty suspects; the servants.

And if the servants didn't turn out to have done it, then perhaps the aforementioned Seagrove or Curry.

Or both of them together.

Morag would've been furious that they would dare to suspect our servant's loyalty, but I suppose they weren't keen to start interviewing the "quality" about their whereabouts.

Inspector Morrison's third shortcoming was to disregard the family, both their beliefs and their knowledge.

As soon as I realised he was going to let the guests go home, I sent the twins lurking in the Ballroom to see who was there, and what they were talking about, and whether anyone said or did anything suspicious.

Fortunately, Mama also sent the older four children to help clear everyone out of the ballroom.

In the meantime, I made myself comfortable in the library while Inspector Morrison started interviewing the staff.

It was clear he rented a full board room in a boarding house; he had no idea how busy a house this size keeps the servants.

Or the amount of time and effort it takes to prepare for a wedding.

Barnes and Mrs Rose the housekeeper were busy supervising the maids and temporary footmen. Even Nanny was pitching in or at least making sure the twins didn't wreck the place.

Or both at the same time.

"Yes, Inspector," Barnes reassured him, "they had *all* been setting up the glasses for champagne and laying out snacks".

Roberts and Prince, Morag's lady's maid, had been together, packing the trunks for the honeymoon.

Dodds the chauffeur had put the car away; no luggage, meant nothing further to do until it was ready to be loaded.

In the meantime, he helped the gardeners lugging the pot plants around in the conservatory for the photographs, and then clearing away the debris.

Once the luggage was ready, one of the gardeners helped him load it up, and in the usual course of events would have helped him unload when they got to Spencer Street Station.

With all the servants alibied out, Inspector Morrison asked whether anyone might have slipped away.

Our servants were too polite to roll their eyes the way I did.

Of course, it was possible. Anyone could have slipped away.

Anyone who didn't want a job anymore at any rate.

Anyone who didn't care about the rest of the household being so busy.

And when you have such a small household, you're generally quite close with the other servants and the family.

I couldn't help wondering why he didn't factor the family into his calculations.

Of course, we were all in the conservatory for the photographs, but he didn't know that.

And just as the servants could slip away, so could the family.

Stephen certainly did, though he only went as far as the Drawing Room for a glass of wine.

Though Mama did frown at him.

As the Inspector took his leave, Mama asked him to look into the whereabouts of Miss Seagrove and Mr Curry.

I wasn't sure he would comply; he was still giving me the vibe of Morag leaving of her own volition.

Mr Smythe came back with the news that there was no sign of Morag in any of the outbuildings and no sign of any suspicious activity.

Barnes discretely handed me the invitation list, in which was recorded the invitees and their RSVPs.

The photographer took his leave, saying the photographs would be available in a week.

We sat in the Drawing Room for a while, but no one said anything. One of the maids brought us tea and some sandwiches.

I was starving, and the twins too.

We ate the sandwiches, but no one else seemed to have much of an appetite.

I suppose it was a big day for them.

Mama went for a lie-down, and my brothers and sisters went their own ways.

I went to check on Henry, and neither he nor Dante seemed to have moved. They were both snoring gently, and Nanny was nowhere to be seen.

Perhaps she'd gone downstairs to the kitchen to be with the other staff.

The twins and I reconvened in the nursery, which had recently been converted into a schoolroom, with had lots of blackboard space.

Space for my lessons, space for Rosanna's lessons, and space for Roland's lessons.

I assumed the Inspector would follow up with interviews of Seagrove and Curry.

I expected he would carry them out away at the police station, and that he would let us know.

Or I suppose more correctly, Henry or Mama.

With the guest list, we had some evidence of who was in the house. We were discussing the people they'd seen when Stephen wandered in to see what we were doing.

It was too late to cover the boards, and I couldn't come up with a reasonable excuse so I told him the truth.

We were trying to work out who had the opportunity to capture Morag.

"Hold on a minute," he said and left the room, reappearing a short while later with all the other children except Henry.

With nine of us together, we started from the beginning - what I had seen and heard.

I didn't have a watch, but through a series of dramatic re-enactments, we concluded you'd need at least four kidnappers to abduct Morag.

Two in the room to subdue her and get her out of the window, two on the ground to catch her and hide in the bushes until I'd left the room.

We estimated perhaps five minutes to accomplish that, and given the Ballroom was on the opposite side of the building, it would be possible to do that out of sight of the guests.

The question was, had I given them enough time to conceal themselves, and I had to admit that the few minutes Dante and I had spent running around the room would have been enough to conceal themselves.

We expected that two people could have abducted her, but it would have taken longer.

It was possible a guest, or guests, had been involved in the kidnapping, but no one noticed any guests who were wetter than the circumstances warranted.

I started to feel quite sad because it was beginning to look as though someone, perhaps Miss Seagrove or Mr Curry, had commissioned the kidnapping.

Nonetheless, we started sorting out the guest list, checking off the expected guests who had been seen, or referred to by other guests.

We were left with a few guests who we couldn't verify.

I decided to check with Barnes to see if he had seen them, and shortly after that, we were able to check them off the list too.

We were left with the option of two or four unknown people, disabling her, and kidnapping her out of her own bedroom.

It was unsupportable.

The next day Inspector Morrison called back at the house to notify us that Miss Seagrove was with her parents at Lakes Entrance, and had been for several months. And Mr Curry had taken the train to Sydney at the beginning of the year.

Neither of them could have known about the wedding.

We were left with no rational explanation for her disappearance.

By lunchtime, Roberts and I bullied Henry out of his bed, and into the bathroom to bathe.

With the door open, Dante ran downstairs, presumably concerned for his own ablutions.

While they were occupied, I picked up Morag's papers from the floor, and I noticed a dark stain on the floor under the desk, I knelt down to see if Dante had left a mess, but it smelled like a burn.

How had it got there?

When I picked up the fountain pen, I notice another, smaller char mark on the carpet, and in some places, the engraving had a kind of drip pattern that I was fairly sure hadn't been there before.

I straightened the papers up on her desk, and naturally, I looked at them.

Her handwriting was atrocious.

There was a list of dates, starting with September 9, 1904, the date she arrived, and followed by August 30, 1905, today's date.

Then a sequence of dates leading up to March 15, 2211. And a separate series of dates ending February 21, 2194. What were the dates about?

There were pages of notes about weather conditions going back several months; freak tornadoes, unexpected snowstorms, and lightning strikes.

Was she perhaps not looking at the news as much as the weather?

And finally, there was a hurried note to Henry, one that broke off mid-sentence.

> *I don't think we got it right. I don't think it was the watch.*
>
> *I think it was an astrological conjunction combined with an unusual weather pattern.*
>
> *If something happens to me, don't try to find me.*
>
> *I'm happy knowing I saved you. I hope you...*

As I said, there was no rational explanation for her disappearance, but was it possible that the same freak conditions that had brought her here, had taken her away again?

It wasn't exactly plausible, but it wasn't exactly implausible either.

And with no rational explanation for Morag's disappearance, we had no option but to believe the unbelievable.

THE END

ABOUT THE AUTHOR

Alexandria Blaelock writes stories, some of them for *Ellery Queen's Mystery Magazine* and *Pulphouse Fiction Magazine*. She's also written four self-help books applying business techniques to personal matters like getting dressed, cleaning house, and feeding your friends.

As a recovering Project Manager, she's probably too fond of sticking to plan. She lives in a forest because she enjoys birdsong, the scent of gum leaves and the sun on her face. When not telecommuting to parallel universes from her Melbourne based imagination, she watches K-dramas, talks to animals, and drinks Campari. At the same time.

Discover more at www.alexandriablaelock.com.

BOOKS BY
ALEXANDRIA BLAELOCK

SHORT STORY COLLECTIONS

The Histories of Hayward Hall
Lovelorn, Lovestruck and Love at First Sight
Common or Garden Variety Heroes
Case Files of the Wilkinson Detective Agency
Unavoidable Fates

OTHER FICTION

That Love Nonsense

MS BLAELOCK'S BOOKS

Stress Free Dinner Parties
Signature Wardrobe Planning
Holistic Personal Finance
Minimally Viable Housekeeping
Planning a Life Worth Living

SELECTED SHORT STORIES

Alma's Grace
Balancing the Book
Carmelita Basingstoke
Fate in Your Hands
Kiss of Death
Lady of the Looking Glass
Life in the Security Directorate
Long Weekend in the Snow
Love in the Past Tense
Love in the Security Directorate
Morning Star, Evening Star, Superstar
Needy Bitch
Payton's Run
Phoenix Child
Secret Singer
Shining Star
Ship in a Bottle
Simone Says Hands in the Air
Special Relativity in Space
The Bygone Boyfriend
The Day the Schedule Broke
The Ghost Detectors
The Guardian's Vigil
The Mince Pie Mystery
The Mystery of the Master Suite
The Pseudonym's Bride
The Shadow Thieves
The Time-Space Paradox
Toy Soldiers

www.ingramcontent.com/pod-product-compliance
Lightning Source LLC
Chambersburg PA
CBHW030814190726
48285CB00003B/1180